little Miss Fickle

by Roger Hargreaves

WORLD INTERNATIONAL

W9-AXZ-487

Would you like me to tell you a story?

If you were Little Miss Fickle,
you'd say, "Yes, please!"
And then you'd say, "No, thank you!"
And then you'd say, "Yes!" again.

Little Miss Fickle was one of those people
who just could not make up their minds.

Ever!

About anything!

Little Miss Fickle lived in Dandelion Cottage which was on the outskirts of Sunnytown.

And she lived right next door to her best friend, Little Miss Neat, who lived in Twopin Cottage.

One Monday, Little Miss Fickle and
Little Miss Neat went out to lunch in Sunnytown.

"I'll have the soup to start with," said
Little Miss Neat to the waiter as she looked
at the menu, "followed by the fish."

"So will I," said Little Miss Fickle.

But after the waiter had written down the order,
Little Miss Fickle looked at the menu again.

"No I won't," she said. "I'll have the salad instead,
followed by the roast chicken!"

The waiter crossed out the first order, and
wrote down the second.

"On the other hand," continued Little Miss Fickle,
"I won't have anything to start with ...
but then I'll have the eggs!"

The waiter sighed.

An hour later, after the waiter had worn out three pencils and four order pads, Little Miss Fickle finally made up her mind to have the soup, followed by the fish.

The waiter brought the soup.

Little Miss Fickle looked at it.
"I'm not hungry any more," she said.

It was at that moment that the waiter decided he was going to be a bus conductor instead of a waiter.

On Tuesday, Little Miss Fickle went to
buy a hat.

"I want a new pink hat," she announced to
the milliner.

The milliner brought her two pink hats
to choose from.

"I'll have this one," said Little Miss Fickle, after
she had tried them both on.

"Certainly, Madam," replied the milliner,
and put the hat in a hatbox.

"On the other hand," said Little Miss Fickle,
"I think I'll have the other hat!"

The milliner took the first hat out of the hatbox ...
and then she put the second hat into the hatbox!

"But," continued Little Miss Fickle, "I think the
first hat suited me better, don't you?"

The milliner didn't say a word as she took the
second hat out of the hatbox ...
and then put the first hat back into the hatbox!

She handed the hatbox to Little Miss Fickle.

Little Miss Fickle looked at the milliner.

"Do you have any blue hats?" she asked.

It was at that moment that the milliner decided she was going to be a ballerina instead of a milliner!

On Wednesday, Little Miss Fickle went to the butcher's.

"I'd like some sausages," she said.

"Beef sausages, or pork sausages?" asked the butcher.

"Pork sausages," replied Little Miss Fickle.

The butcher wrapped up the pork sausages.

"But beef sausages would be nicer," said
Little Miss Fickle.

The butcher unwrapped the pork sausages,
and wrapped up some beef sausages instead.

"On the other hand," continued Little Miss Fickle,
"chops would be tastier!"

It was at that moment that the butcher
decided he needed a holiday.

But, on Thursday, guess what happened?
Little Miss Fickle disappeared!
Little Miss Neat had seen her pass Twopin Cottage
on the way into Sunnytown, but she hadn't come back.

She didn't come back on Friday, either.
So Little Miss Neat went looking for her.

She met Mr Muddle.
"Have you seen Little Miss Fickle?" she
asked anxiously.
Mr Muddle looked at her in a puzzled sort of a way.
"Did you say, 'Have I been for a little tickle?' " he asked.
"Oh, Mr Muddle," said Little Miss Neat, and hurried on.

Then Little Miss Neat met Mr Forgetful.

"Have you seen Little Miss Fickle?" she asked.
Mr Forgetful thought.

"Well," she said, "have you?"
Mr Forgetful thought again.

"Have I what?" he asked, after a while.
"Oh, Mr Forgetful," said Little Miss Neat,
and hurried on.

But could she find Little Miss Fickle?
No, she could not!
Nobody had seen her.

The Sunnytown Public Lending Library has ...
nineteen thousand,
nine hundred,
and ninety-nine books.

On Saturday afternoon, Little Miss Fickle reached up
and took one of them down from a shelf.

"I'll read this one," she thought to herself.

"On the other hand," she thought again, looking at
another book, "perhaps I'll read that book instead!"

She put the first book back on the shelf,
and took the other book down.

It was the nineteen thousand,
nine hundred,
and ninety-ninth book she had chosen!

Little Miss Fickle had been in the library for three
days choosing a book.

Three whole days choosing just one single,
solitary book!

She went home carrying her book.

That Saturday afternoon, Little Miss Neat was in the garden of Twopin Cottage when Little Miss Fickle walked past.

"Where have you BEEN?" she called out.

"To the library," replied Little Miss Fickle.

"For THREE days?" exclaimed Little Miss Neat.

"Well," explained Little Miss Fickle,
"I wanted to choose the right book!"

And she held it up.
And then she stopped and looked at it.

"Oh, botherations!" she said.
"I've read it before!"

SPECIAL OFFERS FOR MR MEN AND LITTLE MISS READERS

In every Mr Men and Little Miss book you will find a special token. Collect only six tokens and we will send you a super poster of your choice featuring all your favourite Mr Men or Little Miss friends.

And for the first 4,000 readers we hear from, we will send you a Mr Men activity pad* and a bookmark* as well – absolutely free!

Return this page with six tokens from Mr Men and/or Little Miss books to:
Marketing Department, World International Limited, Deanway Technology Centre, Wilmslow Road, Handforth, Cheshire SK9 3FB.

Your name:_____

Address:_____

_____

_____ Postcode: _____

Signature of parent or guardian: _____

I enclose **six** tokens – please send me a Mr Men poster ☐
I enclose **six** tokens – please send me a Little Miss poster ☐

We may occasionally wish to advise you of other children's books that we publish. If you would rather we didn't, please tick this box ☐

*while stocks last   (Please note: this offer is limited to a maximum of two posters per household.)

Collect six of these tokens. You will find one inside every Mr Men and Little Miss book which has this special offer.

1 TOKEN

Please remove this page carefully

Join the

MR.MEN & little miss
Club

Treat your child to membership of the long-awaited Mr Men & Little Miss Club and see their delight when they receive a personal letter from Mr Happy and Little Miss Giggles, a club badge **with their name on**, and a superb Welcome Pack. And imagine how thrilled they'll be to receive a card from the Mr Men and Little Misses on their birthday and at Christmas!

Take a look at all of the great things in the Welcome Pack, every one of them of superb quality (*see box right*). If it were

on sale in the shops, the Pack alone would cost around £12.00. But a year's membership, including all of the other Club benefits, costs just **£7.99** (plus 70p postage) with a 14 day money-back guarantee if you're not delighted.

To enrol your child please send **your** name, address and telephone number together with **your child's** full name, date of birth and address (including postcode) and a cheque or postal order for £8.69 (payable to Mr Men & Little Miss Club) to: Mr Happy, Happyland (Dept. WI), PO Box 142, Horsham RH13 5FJ. Or call 01403 242727 to pay by credit card.

Please note: We reserve the right to change the terms of this offer (including the contents of the Welcome Pack) at any time but we offer a 14 day no-quibble money-back guarantee. We do not sell directly to children - all communications (except the Welcome Pack) will be via parents/guardians. After 31/12/96 please call to check that the price is still valid. Please allow 28 days for delivery. Promoter: Robell Media Promotions Limited, registered in England number 2852153.

The Welcome Pack:

✓ Membership card
✓ Personalized badge
✓ Club members' cassette with Mr Men stories and songs
✓ Copy of Mr Men magazine
✓ Mr Men sticker book
✓ Tiny Mr Men flock figure
✓ Personal Mr Men notebook
✓ Mr Men bendy pen
✓ Mr Men eraser
✓ Mr Men book mark
✓ Mr Men key ring

Plus:

✓ Birthday card
✓ Christmas card
✓ Exclusive offers
✓ Easy way to order Mr Men & Little Miss merchandise

All for just £7·99! (plus 70p postage)